BECAUSE I WANTED TO
WRITE YOU A POP SONG

BECAUSE I WANTED TO WRITE YOU A POP SONG

Stories by
Kara Vernor

Split Lip Press

Published by Split Lip Press
333 Sinkler Road
Wyncote, PA 19095
www.splitlippress.com

ISBN: 978-0-9909035-7-4

Cover Design by Ken Prosser
Cover Art by Kim Miscowicz
http://kimmiskowicz.com/

Dedicated to
My Mother
and
Guy Biederman

TABLE OF CONTENTS

SHE COULD MAYBE
LIFT A CAR

WHEN YOU WALK into a party with blood on your face, well, people will think it's your blood. Funny how that works. Like clothes and perfume. If you're wearing it, it must yours. My friends were looking at me like, *Oh my god, What happened to you?* Like maybe my boyfriend punched me with that skull ring of his. He was known for that ring, and his ability to pin guys in unitards in less than twenty seconds.

People were assuming. What they didn't know was my shirt (satin with daisies), it was my friend Jenny's; the blood (sticky and bright), my boyfriend Rick's. So I told them. I held up my hand and said, "It's not my blood," but everyone kept staring, their red cups somewhere between their waists and their mouths.

"It's not my blood," I said again, but of course they were still wondering. I was no help; I wasn't ready to confess.

I went to the bathroom and washed my face. The blood streamed to the sides, and I had to shove a hand towel deep into my earholes to get it out. It's funny how last night I was sipping Raspberry Zinger and studying the quadratic equation, where tonight I am covered in blood. My mom says not to run off with the first guy I meet because he could have chlamydia, or an addiction to internet porn, or impotence. Guys can bypass dating with mail order brides from Russia, she says. There are no mail order husbands.

Rick had told me I looked "a little slutty" when we walked up to the party. I said, "Give me a break, it's not even my shirt." I tried to hold his hand but he pulled away. I said, "Isn't it perfect how Rick rhymes with dick." That's when he shoved me to the grass.

The good news is, I am likely a secret ninja, because when Rick the Dick lunged at me for more, I kicked fast, like a rabbit on its back, which is kind of crazy because *kick first, ask questions later* is not what they teach in school. Lessons aside though, you don't know what you can do on adrenaline. You could maybe lift a car.

My heel snapped his nose and it sounded like a plum splattering. He came down on me still but was impaired. I'm sure he thought he was teaching me a lesson, pinning me down, hanging his busted plum nose over my face, letting it drip, drip, drip. I agree, it was unpleasant: rolling down my neck and pooling in my eyes. I shut them tighter. I thought *his, not mine*, which is how I prefer it. Not my blood.

People are knocking at the door now, saying, "Hey, are you okay in there?"

"Yes," I say, "I'll be out in a minute."

They're saying, "Hey, where's Rick?"

I look myself over once more. Jenny's shirt is ruined, but otherwise I look good—hair fluffed, lips pink and glossy. I look ready to open the door to a house full of guys I haven't yet dated. I'm thinking I could maybe date a gold medal mathlete. I could make out with a Russian spy.

THE RUMOR WAS

THREE PEOPLE HAD DIED on the rollercoaster, each decapitated by a wooden plank. He told her this as the lap bar lowered over them and locked. "Their ghosts haunt the tunnel," he said, and the attendant threw the lever. The car jerked forward, dropping them in.

The rumor was a scared girl was an easy girl. Fear made her pull him closer, lace her fingers through his. He led her back to the line seven times until, dizzy and sour-mouthed, she broke away, steadied herself over a steel drum, and gagged. He wrapped his sweatshirt around her shoulders and walked her to the beach.

The rumor was the beach was where it happened. Lips parted, tongues shot out, hands slid under sweaters, wedged beneath waistbands. They sat below the wharf and talked about nothing, the nothing people talk about when they're waiting.

The rumor was this is what boys did to girls. When she liked it, liked it so much she initiated acts with her mouth he had not expected, he stiffened accordingly, but his mind rushed. Was he to lay back, to moan, to fill his eyes with the moon? Like a girl?

The rumor was it went as planned. A lot of tongue kissing and a warm tit in each hand. He didn't mention the thing with her mouth. He didn't mention his banging heart, a car loose from its track. The building and building, salt air in and out of his lungs, the top approaching. The top, where he threw his hands up and screamed.

BECAUSE I WANTED TO WRITE YOU A POP SONG

JOHNNY CALLS ME his Numero Uno groupie. I call me his girlfriend. We've been together since Sarah Loquat's graduation party a few months back. We were both single and bored and sitting on the same couch. You know how that goes. I remind him he doesn't have any groupies. He tucks my hair behind my ear and says, *Yeah, but I got you babe.*

Johnny's got a problem with the "L" word, except in his songs. In his songs he loves a lot of people: Karla, Leena, Farrah, Sue, even Eric. I gave him a yard sale t-shirt—navy and orange from a 1973 folk festival— that I thought might make him love me in a song. The way he looked at me after he tried it on, like I had turned from cubic zirconium to actual diamond, I swear it almost worked. But all he did was kiss my head and pat my butt and say, *Ooh, ooh, tangled up in blue.*

After my dad stole the family car and left us in Bakersfield, my mom tried to pawn her wedding ring. That's how she learned it was CZ. Shit was fake, she told me. She dropped it in her leftover mashed potatoes and tossed it in the trash at the KFC. I thought, You know what? It still looked pretty.

If Johnny's got another girl, she's way part-time, as in more part-time than his job at the laundromat. I know because I'm always around. Or he's playing a gig and I'm around then, too. I asked him the other day to be sure. We had had sex on his futon and he hadn't fallen asleep yet. He said, Uno—he calls me that for short—he said, *Dream up, dream up, let me fill your cup.* Then he farted in front of me for the first time, which was almost as good as I love you when you think about how it meant we were definitely a couple.

When Johnny's not around, I listen to music I don't tell him about: Michael Jackson, Justin Timberlake, Katy Perry. Sometimes a girl has to dance. Still, I start ukulele lessons because it's sexy and different, and I have a dream of playing instrumental versions of all of Johnny's favorite folks songs on the ukulele. Bands would invite me open for them, though I would never get a record deal.

I practice the ukulele with the hit song, "Call Me Maybe." When Johnny walks in on me playing it, he says, "Dude, not cool." He plants himself on my couch, rolls a cigarette, lights it with his Zippo, and then puffs his way out the door. What I want to know is, how did he recognize the song,

My mom likes to say the best couples grow together, so after mastering some ukulele basics, I decide to present Johnny with a growth opportunity. Maybe he needs to dance? I write my very own ukulele original, a pop number inspired by the night I met him. I record it on my mom's handheld cassette player so I can play it in on a boom box outside his window like the guy in that '80s movie. Johnny loves anything vintage.

"Uno?" he says after I call his name and hit play. "Is that you?"

He leans out his window, lights a cigarette and listens for a bit.

My arms get tired but I persist.

He says, "You know what, Uno? You should have learned '50 Ways to Leave Your Lover.'" Then he shuts the window and lowers the blinds.

The thing is, I like that song too, I do. But now I won't get to tell him. I'll never get to tell him I do.

When I get home I can't go to sleep. I lie there thinking about Johnny, remembering the art opening we went to at the coffee shop next to the laundromat. Each painting was the size of a postcard, but looking at them—dark blue backdrop with different colored specks and dots—they were windows to outer space. I was talking loud, I guess, saying, "Don't you wish you were inside of them? Don't they make you feel so small?"

He said, "Shhhhh," and gave me a look. Then he walked away and left me thinking about all the galaxies that aren't ours, all the planets we could live on but never will.

BETTY

IF YOU'D MET my Grandma Betty, you'd remember. A senior citizen who thinks herself a coed, she wears Jordache jeans. She pulls her hair back with a headband. The Alibi loves Grandma Betty.

They get her talking. They get her take on final scores. She knows football, boxing, rugby, and curling, and can calculate a batting average during the second between the game and the commercial break. She says cycling today is an embarrassment of chemistry. She wishes they would go back to smoking.

Grandma Betty is a rooter like no other. She watches from the diamond-tucked bench of the round booth, a pitcher of Hamm's and a hot dog on the table in front of her. It's a perfect view of both big screen TVs. When two games are on, she roots for all four teams, wearing the colors of each randomly, like a rack at a thrift store. Once on Christmas when the Bengals played the Vikings, she showed up as a tiger with horns.

They think she's always been there.

The times I've joined her, I've seen her eyes drift toward the door. A few years back I found a suitcase in her trunk, packed in who knows which decade, with a bathing suit, a plastic lei, Bermuda shorts and a bible. A photo of a young man with a dead buck. When I asked her about it she said you just never know.

They can spot her coming and going, her Chevelle rolling like a lazy eye too far to the right. They think it's from the drinking, but they would think that. I think she hasn't made up her mind. Stay or go.

FERRIS WHEEL

IT SEEMED LIKE a good place to meet. It was public; violence was unlikely. In front of this looming, spinning backdrop, she waited, the wind whipping her trench coat against her knees. Was this real, or a movie she had once seen? One of many she watched while crocheting on the orange shag, her father cleaning rifles at the kitchen table. On screen her heels were taller, her hair longer. But perhaps this was the autumn light.

Ten minutes past four.

"Hey lady, you want to take a ride?"

She paid the boy with a handful of change from the bottom of her purse. As the car lifted her up and away, she inhaled the sea. The people below grew smaller, and she felt like Fay Wray suspended in King Kong's hand. He had been gentle, he had wanted to keep her safe. Below, she wondered which speck was or was not wild to find her.

CRASH

THAT TIME ON A HIGHWAY in a cold part of California. The car in front of mine hit its brakes, hard. So I hit my brakes, hard. The redwoods looming, the raindrops hovering. And this one pale woman sailing over the first car toward my windshield, her chin wrenched past her shoulder, her one eye meeting mine like she wanted a witness.

FOUR HANDS

JANEY WANTS ME to teach her to pray. She's never been to church, only seen inside of one on her TV, so she kneels by my bed and presses her palms together. "Like this, right?"

Janey has the longest, blackest hair in all of fifth grade. She's also the biggest bitch. I'm onto this, how the longer your hair is, the meaner you are. I cut mine at my shoulders, so I can go either way. Janey's runs the center of her back, a slick, braided spine. In my dreams it's the rope we yank in tug-of-war, a tree swing that slips free, one I stretch after as I lift into the air, through the hole in the ozone layer, and into the black.

Janey has a lot of reasons to pray, but right now she's after an A in math. An A comes with a Hello Kitty cruiser and pink helmet to match, her mom promised. Her mom, who is best friends with my mom since they met the first day of high school and began saving together for their dream car, a purple Trans Am. My mom makes me go to church and Janey's makes her go to ballet, and usually we both think she has the better deal, but Janey's not sure now given her problem with numbers, how she can't understand them on the right side of the dot. She flips her braid over her shoulder and waves me closer.

"Talking to God is going to be a lot easier than me learning decimals."

She takes my hands and flattens them between hers, like four hands are better at praying than two, like it's as simple as math she understands.

Janey thinks I'm good with God because of my trip last summer to Circus Circus, where my mom had set my brothers and me loose on the games floor, each of us thumbing a roll of quarters in our pocket. Now Janey wants to hear it again.

"Just the part about the Ring-a-Bottle," she says. "I don't care how many times your brothers farted in the car."

I say how the moment I laid eyes on the game, it felt like time bent. Like someone muted the TV and put it on slow-mo. All the mouths in the middle of words. I pushed up to the counter with my last quarters, and with the three rings they paid for, I crossed myself—I can't say why. When I looked out over the table of glass bottles, I knew the first ring would catch, knew it like my grandma knew my grandpa had been hit by a minivan, like my mom knew about my dad and his dental hygienist. After

18

it happened, I pointed at the prize above my head—a panther, almost as tall as me, with thick fangs and no privates. Janey thinks the holiest part is how I dream different with it in my room. Instead of tarantulas in my rain boots and snakes slithering into my bed, it's me losing at tetherball, a little bit of going to school naked. Embarrassing, maybe, but nothing that will kill me.

Janey's at the end of my dresser now, peering into the panther's eyes, her nose inches from its fangs. At a middle school party a few weeks ago she tongue-kissed her older brother's friend, so things like fangs don't scare her anymore.

"Show me how to make the cross," she says.

I'm still sore at her for last weekend, when she planted an eyeliner on me in CVS and didn't tell me until we got home. I've got no good reason to do what she says.

"What if it wasn't God? What if it was Circus Circus?" I say. "Did I tell you about the lady in the leotard riding the man in leather who was riding a motorcycle inside a cage *in the air*? Anything could happen there."

"What if?" Janey says, running her hand over my panther's back. "What if I tell everyone you still wet the bed like a baby?"

I don't, but that won't stop her from saying it.

"Huh, bed-wetter, how about that?"

See? Biggest bitch.

I push her back to the bed and onto her knees.

"All right then," I say, and I go for it: "Close your eyes. Talk to

God in your head. Say please a lot. Tell him everything you've ever done that's bad and ask for forgiveness. Better say it out loud so I can tell if you say it right."

She closes her eyes but then pops one open to look at me.

"Well, go on," I say, my face straight.

She arranges her prayer hands in front of her heart and starts, starts so hard her forehead goes ugly with wrinkles. She's saying dear god forgive me, forgive me for switching costumes on Halloween and hitting all the houses twice, for peeing on my brother's toothbrush when he shoots my Barbies with his air gun, for wiping boogers under Julie Mell's desk and telling everyone she's a nose-picker.

"You think that's good?" Janey asks.

"Maybe a little more to make sure. You really want the bike, right?"

She keeps on, about putting dog poo in her neighbor's mailbox and how she killed a salamander because she was curious. She's clicking her heels together as fast as she's talking, her palms pressing flatter, and I'm thinking how if her dad were here, he'd slap her for all of it, send that braid flying, because maybe somebody should. But he's been gone for a year and she still says he's on vacation in Aruba. I'm about to tell her that's enough when her voice catches and her face twists up like her forehead.

"*And no one likes me,*" she says loud. It's the sound that sets off a landslide. One boulder, then another, then a whole house crashes down. What follows is harder to understand because she's mad and sad and red and starting to slobber.

"Why did you make me so mean?" she says finally, sucking for air.

I've seen plenty of Janey's fake crying, but this real crying is awful. It's my dream in reverse where now I'm on earth and she's the one slipping into the dark. I feel a fire growing in my throat.

"Put your head down," I say, and I sit behind her. I slip off the rubber band at the end of her braid, and work my fingers through until it loosens and her hair tents around her and makes her look small. Then I brush it slowly while she sniffles, and I feel glad for not having to see her face.

"That thing with the salamander, that's not okay."

"I know."

"And dog poo? That's just gross."

"Are you going to tell anybody?"

"No."

I move next to her and put my palms together. My room feels strange, like it might be in orbit; it might be on its way to Mars. With the curtains drawn I don't know if it's my backyard out there or a black hole. I close my eyes and see Janey and I at our prom, Janey with this blue satin dress and these huge boobs. I see us smoking cigarettes in a bar with deer heads on all the walls and guns mounted everywhere in between. I see Janey parked on a cliff above the ocean, her head bent over the steering wheel, her black hair cut jagged and blunt. It's that feeling again, that I know what comes next. I wrap an arm around her shoulder and whisper, "Hold on to me."

PROM QUEEN FOUND IN LAKE

SHE BOUGHT a black dress with a gold sequined bust. She pressed on nails and singed her hair into curls. He liked red lipstick and she wore red lipstick. He liked Southern Comfort and she shoplifted a bottle. She convinced everyone to pitch in for a limo so he could fake like a rock star, so he could pop out of the roof, stretch his arms wide, and sing, "Please allow me to introduce myself," the moon strobing through the sugar pines.

At the dance she was the sun and he was a planet in need of heat. During slow songs his fingernails bit into her nape, his hand with its own language, saying, *Closer, I will combust for you.* When they posed for the picture, he picked her up like a new bride, her face flushed and shiny, his mouth at her ear. It was this photo that circulated during the search.

After hours in the interrogation room, the photo between them, the detective thought to ask, "What was it you were you saying to her?"

He rubbed his eyes with the heels of his palms, leaned back into his chair. "Christ, what would you have said? I mean, look at her." He nestled his arms across his chest. "I told her, 'Baby, you are way too hot.'"

*Lyrics from "Sympathy for the Devil" by Jagger/Richards

DON JOHNSON IS NOT
YOUR MAN

STEPHAN WORKS at the cookie store in the mall. It's how he gets gas money and chicks. He has a Honda CR-X with a spoiler, but he almost never gives me a ride, even when mom tells him to.

"Sonny Crockett would not work in a mall," I tell him.

He grabs me by the collar and rubs his armpit all over my head.

Still, I ask him questions when I have to because who else can I ask? Yesterday I asked about how you can't smell vodka on the breath. Myth or fact, I wanted to know. Today I'm thinking of asking if boys like to have sex with girls on their periods. But maybe I'll think of something else.

Stephan has two white blazers he wears with pastel t-shirts. I tell him pink only looks good on black guys, and he tells me to shut up.

25

"What do you know about black guys," he says.

I found a bottle of self-tanner in his gym bag but gave him a break on that one. Cincinnati is no Miami.

The nice thing he used to do for me was bring home cookies. My favorite is chocolate chip, no walnuts. But now that he's selling cocaine too, he doesn't remember about the cookies.

The other night he came home drunk, which I could tell because he talked wrong. He threw a wad of cash into the middle of my room and told me I could have it.

"I don't deserve it," he said, but it sounded like *I doan jasurve it.*

Then he lay down on the floor and didn't get back up. It was my brother passed out on all this money.

I don't know what he was thinking those nights we watched *Miami Vice*. Crockett and Tubbs were cops, not dealers. It reminds me of how he walks around singing that Dire Straights song like, *Baby get a pistol on your little finger/Baby get a pistol on your thumb.*

It's maybe, not baby, I tell him. Blister, not pistol.

THIRTY-FOUR

WHEN DONNIE TOLD ME I couldn't look more beautiful, he wasn't saying it to be nice. He was saying I was a peach on the day it falls from the tree.

"I'm not giving you kids yet," I told him. "You can't scare me into it."

He knows the deal.

I said, "If you want kids, quit working at the bar."

Later I walked downtown to see a movie, a romance between a bartender who is deathly allergic to alcohol and a pretty, hard-drinking research scientist. It's all carnival rides and mini-golf until the bartender sips the scientist's gin-spiked ginger ale. I guessed all five of us in the audience saw this coming. The scientist rushes to the lab and develops a cure just in time to save him. Hollywood ending: check. When the usher asked me how it was, I gave him a horizontal thumb. I thought the movie might help me understand Donnie and me, but he's a bartender who drinks, I got a C in chemistry, and not once did that movie bartender dump the pretty lady's birth control pills in the toilet tank to be discovered later by the lady when the water in the bowl turned pink.

Walking home I saw myself in the window of a beauty salon: my hair parted down the middle, hanging in two flaps. I thought to shave them off and hang them behind the wheels of a semi-truck. I have a feeling if I were bald people wouldn't say things like, *You'd make a good mom*. They wouldn't say, *What are you waiting for?*

When my car died last week, a semi with wheel flaps picked me up and drove me back to Kansas City. I wanted the driver to know things I didn't. Like why my cat Wilma rejected one of her kittens and if free will is a thing. He talked about the Chiefs and curing meat, kind of like a lot of guys. When I stepped out at the Flying J, I hadn't learned anything that would help me leave the man I love while I still loved him.

If I were a peach, and I'm not saying I am, I might like life after the fall, the ants crawling over me, the sun baking my skin, my flesh cracking open, revealing the pit inside. There would be no decision in it. No Donnie and his Irish coffee breath, no preoccupation with the unevenness of his face, no wondering if his smell means our immune systems are different enough to make strong babies. Just the slow turn of the sun in the sky, the sprout breaking through me, a small pressure.

WEREWOLVES

SHE SLEEPS WITH her BB gun next to her bed. On hot nights, she touches the cool metal to her legs. When she can't sleep, she flips it end to end like a rain stick and listens. Roger said when he gave it to her: "Don't point it at anyone ever, whether it's loaded or not." Her mom said: "One mistake and that gun is gone."

This is Saturday. Roger sits across the table forking wet eggs. There is a dribble of yellow on his white shirt and a spot of shine on his chest hair, that V of forest canopy. It's lusher and darker than the patch beneath her panties. She can't help but stare.

"What are you looking at," he says, and she turns her eyes to the salt. Her mother eats standing at the counter, refilling orange juice before being asked.

In the empty house next door, she and her brother shoot soda cans off the fireplace mantle.

"We're practicing our aim," she says.

She loads the gun for him and he points and clicks, his face pure glee when the first can topples off.

"Again," he calls, and she sets up a new configuration, one that will crumble and clatter more fantastically when hit.

It is an accident when her brother shoots himself in the neck, the BB ricocheting off the bricks.

"It's okay," she tells him. "It's alright."

She holds him on the blue carpet, her hand lodged over his cries. Her mother is nearby, out back with the chickens. When his breathing stops backfiring, she settles on what she has to do. She moves over him and pins him with her hands and knees, her hair falling into his face.

She says, "Don't tell mom. Not a word."

She says, "If you tell mom, I'll let the werewolves know how to find you. Next full moon and ssssttt." She runs a finger across her throat.

After dinner Roger pulls her to him as he watches TV, as her mom folds laundry in the bedroom. He pushes her head against his chest and his hands wander. They haven't made it to the soft spot at the base of her V, not yet. At the base of his, right below her chin, is his heart. She can hear it regurgitating, persisting, and she thinks on one thing: stilling it with the tip of her gun. (*Hold it there, hands up!*) Pushing into that soft spot before he can push into hers.

The next day her brother won't talk to her, so she drags him to the corner store and buys him an ice cream sandwich.

"I'm sorry," she says. "Please take it."

She sits with him on the curb. Halfway through he stops shrugging off her arm, and as he finishes the last bite, he leans into her.

She says, "Cross my heart, I will never let anyone hurt you."

"Next weekend?" he asks.

"Yes, we'll shoot again. As much as you want."

That night she flips her gun back and forth and grows tired, the BBs pattering out a whisper, the whisper turning into a lullaby.

USUALLY ON SUNDAY

I LET HIM ring the doorbell eleven times. I knew he knew I was home, and I knew he wanted my eggs.

"You must have a stockpile," he said when I opened the door. He hadn't been by last week.

With the breeze pushing past me I asked him, "What is it about chainsaws on Sundays?" I could smell gasoline on the wind. "You wait here," I told him and took his empty carton.

It's true, I can't eat all of the eggs my two hens lay. Even with salsa and cheddar, I tire of the texture. Even between two slices of sourdough. So I throw them instead. I fill up a basket, pedal by moonlight to the beach and anchor my bike in the sand. From the edge of the shore with my feet stinging cold, I throw them one by one into the dark. I don't know for sure, but I don't think they break. I think they float and confuse the gulls who see nothing but the whites of eyes. A school of dead whales.

Dr. Montgomery caught me one time, he and his Doberman. He caught me on a night when I was angry and throwing against the rocks of the jetty. Little popping skulls. The Doctor told me he is a lover of eggs, but also, why would I hurl them with such force? When they are so delicate to begin with?

Now he comes by each week so nothing goes to waste. And also because he doesn't want anything to break. I have twelve eggs to give him today.

"I've been missing the beach," I say, and he's extra thankful for the full carton. When he gets home he'll see only eleven are whole, that one has a gash in its side.

BONUS ROUND

AND THEN ONE DAY your molester turns up as a contestant on *Wheel of Fortune*. He's standing at his station clapping as the wheel he just tugged spins. He's gray now and liver-spotted, but it's the same man who lived four houses down from your parents until sometime, while you were away at college, he moved.

When you regularly watched *Wheel of Fortune* you were not the age you are now—the age of meeting friends for walks in the hills, which is what you'll do after you eat your chana masala and feed your cat. You were not the age when you met friends for cheap beers and angry bands, nor the age when you gathered by the loading dock behind the mall to share cigarettes. You were the age when being with friends required adult supervision, except on your street where you could play in driveways but not inside, though you sometimes went inside when you thought nobody was home. You lived with your parents then, four split-levels and an empty lot down from Mr. Gorman. You remember now. The lot, too. It's where you fell on a steel can and sliced your knee. Four stitches was all it took, but the pain, how you howled.

He solves a Before & After with "There Will Be Blood Pressure." He points as he says it, stresses each syllable. Then Pat Sajak is next to him, shaking his hand. Pat looks like he did on your parents' TV, chipper and bronzed, but Gorman, he's a shrinking man. A deflated balloon. You see his hand shake the next time he reaches for the wheel, the same hand he pretended wasn't touching between your legs as he talked of his new sailboat, the maiden voyage he would take to Sausalito. He looks like someone you might extend an elbow to if you saw him at an intersection, if he hadn't caught you in his house with his hands, if he hadn't pulled you onto his lap in his Barcalounger, promising not to tell your parents about your sneaking...*if*. His spin clicks to a stop a notch away from Bankrupt, and he lets out a sigh.

You shut off the TV and sit there remembering old thoughts of nailing his hands to the hull of his boat, of loosing it into a storm. Then you get up and bring your plate to the kitchen because you have that walking date with a friend, and you are the age when that's the perfect way to spend the evening. You don't smoke anymore, you don't drink until you throw up, you don't wake from dreams of suffocating under sails, you don't even avoid the ocean. You pay your rent on time, you have a boyfriend who tells math jokes, you have a job that builds you more than it breaks you, and at some point along the way, you did loose that boat. You don't need the TV to show you Rob Gorman is as good as dead.

WINE COUNTRY

THE OTHER DAY a man knocked at my door. He was white and seemed nice enough. I don't think a mean man would wear a beige jumpsuit. It was a little rude when he pushed me aside and demanded food, but I too get crabby when I'm hungry.

He dug into the cheese plate I arranged and asked if I ever thought about dying. I told him yes, sometimes, but what a morbid question. Why was he so morbid?

Turns out he had escaped from the Napa State Hospital for the Criminally Insane. It's really quite a beautiful facility, though tourists tend to skip it. I suggested the facility add a tasting room to attract visitors. They could paint it Desert Sand or Rustic Brown or Slate Gray. My new friend liked Slate Gray.

He then explained he was on his way to heaven to be with Jesus. He said heaven is a movie theater in Tacoma, Washington, and his date with Jesus was Thursday at 3:00 pm.

Before he left, he tied me up and stuffed me in the closet. He also urinated on me despite there being a perfectly good half-bathroom next to the kitchen. I forgave him since he hadn't kept polite company in some time.

It took me a few hours to untie myself, at which point I showered, poured a glass of Sauvignon Blanc, and sat on the patio. I sat there thinking about primary colors, of all things, and how much I missed them.

LESBIONIC

WORKING AT Hamburger Hut when you're a meth addict and a lesbian is just like working at Hamburger Hut when you're a meth addict. But you can't tell Cassie that. She thinks being gay makes her special, makes her "lesbionic" she says and flexes her bicep, the one with the inked portrait of Jesse James.

She leaves me alone. I'm pear-shaped and she likes apples. I'm dirty blonde and she likes them clean. She wants Sabrina, with her perky ponytail, her cute-enough-to-be-a-counter-girl confidence. I work the fryer, and maybe that's not glamorous but I'm good at it, so good that when Cassie disappears to snort lines off the toilet tank, I also cover the grill. Multi-tasking, says my career counselor at the JC, is a transferable skill, one crucial in my future field, emergency medical services. No one puts "pretty" on a resume. No one puts "laughs at lame jokes if you bench-press 275," which is all I can tell Sabrina is good for.

Cassie's habit makes her the best employee or the worst. She cleans the grill in half the time it would take a strongman or she fucks-off and leaves it for the morning shift. I stay behind and clean up for her because I'm that kind of friend, one who steps up when needed. "Steps up when needed," my counselor is going to like that. Plus, it's hard to be mad at Cassie. I like guys and all, but she has this dimple that comes out when she smiles. Gets me every time. I imagine her in an old-timey photo, cigarette dangling from her mouth, pistols at her hips. And I want to be there, too, the girl in the corset, or maybe just the horse.

We're locking up when Cassie asks Sabrina if she needs a ride to the Dump—that's what we call it. It's really a field on top of a hill next to the dump where the air is foul but the cops never come.

"You know I got a ride," she says. Her chariot is a truck with wheels up to my tits, doors so high you need to pole vault your way in. We watch from Cassie's LeBaron as a guy in a cowboy hat reaches across the passenger seat to help lift Sabrina inside.

"He's obviously compensating," I say. Cassie pulls up behind the truck and tails them.

The Dump is the Dump: a keg, a bonfire, a car stereo turned all the way up. People we met in grade school, including Javier with his BB guns, shooting at empties in the firelight. Cassie takes a turn, knocks down six in a row like no big deal. Someone passes her a joint while people hoot at her shooting, but she's a dumbass and looks to see if Sabrina's looking. She's not. Then again, who am I to talk? I'm nursing a Coors Light, reciting lines from *Anchorman* and *The Hangover* with Gabe Allard, a guy known for being able to put his own dick in his mouth. That's been the rumor since seventh grade. We leave eventually, drive by the big box parking lots, but nothing's going on. Cassie drops me home, and I fall asleep to a rerun of *Grey's Anatomy*.

I don't bug Cassie about the drugs—we've been close just four months since she started at the Hut, and she's the best friend I've got now that Karlee left for college. But I can't also hold my tongue about Sabrina, how she's begun joining Cassie in the bathroom. "We'll be with you shortly," I get used to calling from the fryer because I cannot be in three places at once, though that would be even better for my resume, for my future career. I will one day be equipped to revive Cassie should she get a bad batch, but a defibrillator won't fix her lack of common sense. "Sabrina's using you," I blurt out during our nightly smoke break. "She doesn't talk to you when her boyfriend's around, you know?"

"That's because she wants to get on this," Cassie says and runs a display hand across her torso. "If she gets too close, the cow-tipper will catch on." Cassie says she's been fooling with Sabrina in the bathroom, second-basing it is all. Sabrina stops her after a couple of minutes, says she's worried truck boy will find out, says she's not really a dyke. As if that needs saying.

"And if she tells her boyfriend? Says it's your fault? You'd better go into hiding."

"I know you want to help, but you need to quit worrying about me and get your own self laid." She takes a drag, watches me.

"I've been laid before." Cassie raises her eyebrows. "Serious, I've laid, like, two guys. Did oral on another."

Cassie laughs. "Did oral, huh? We should be calling you the Hut Slut."

I try to give her my hard face.

Cassie runs out of meth and starts looking rained on. Mud puddles collect under her eyes and the old oil seeps up from her pores, the slick as thick as Vaseline. She keeps her hands in her pockets for the shaking, like someone chilled through. And the mistakes—dropping meat patties on the floor, forgetting to add pickles, sneezing all over the vegetable vats.

It's in this state she has her accident. She's rolling a dolly stacked high with boxes of cheese when she slips and ends up in a tangle on the floor, the dolly's crossbar handle biting down before she can get clear of it. She sits up, holds her hand in front of her face, and watches as blood lavas down her middle finger. "But I..." she says and passes out against the condiment packet cabinet. I tie off her finger with an apron string, call 911, and then look for her fingertip, which has rolled beneath the register, fingernail attached. It's a small bit given all that blood, but I wash it off and put it in a cup with crushed ice just in case. I may not be a paramedic yet, but watch enough hospital dramas and you pick up a thing or two. Turns out my efforts are in vain, and a plastic surgeon has to take a chunk of Cassie's ass to make her finger whole again. Good thing she's still on her mom's insurance.

Since then Cassie's been trying to quit using, says the accident got her thinking about the drugs and what they do to her. "It could have been worse," she says flipping a row of sesame buns. "Could have been my nose. I would have had ass at the end of my nose."

"Brown-noser," I say. That's how it is now, all ass jokes all the time because they're the only thing that will bring out her dimple.

Things are different between Cassie and Sabrina, of course. "What's her deal?" Cassie asks. She honestly doesn't know.

"Her deal is she likes dick," I say.

Cassie won't let it go, and a few days later, fueled by what I'd guess is a morning fix, she arrives in full swagger, rearing to take another run at Barbie, which is exactly what she does, angling closer, arm propped up on the milkshake machine, talking Sabrina up until pretty soon she's got her laughing, got her coming back between customers for more. I start thinking Cassie *is* lesbionic—she's going to turn Sabrina right here in the middle of Hamburger Hut, the two of them inching closer together. Cassie makes her move, reaches out and rests a hand on Sabrina's waist. Sabrina flinches.

"Stop it."

"Sorry." Cassie jerks her chin toward the back. "Bathroom?"

"You carrying?"

"Nah, I'm trying to quit."

Sabrina turns her back to Cassie, flips her ponytail over her shoulder and starts refilling the napkin dispensers.

"Sabrina?" Cassie says. She says it again, and then one more time: "Sabrina." No response. Cassie stands there looking out the front window, her head calculating. With her face slack she looks younger, looks as naïve as she's been acting, and I think of her as a little kid, when she didn't put gel in her hair, or have tattoos, or know how to smoke drugs out of a bottle cap. She probably played with Barbies of her own, or maybe Tonka trucks. And here she was in a world still stuck like that: it's pink or blue, or you'd better be tough.

Cassie itches her nose with the back of her hand, starts to walk away. I want to grab Sabrina by the ponytail, drag her out the front door and push her into traffic. Show her how it feels to be so easily flattened. Before turning the corner into the kitchen, Cassie stops, swivels back, and extends her mast of a middle finger.

"You know what, Sabrina?" she says. "You can go ahead and kiss my ass." Then she struts out the backdoor, revs the LeBaron, and peels out onto 3rd Street.

The next day I give my two-weeks notice. I'm not about to work at the Hut without Cassie, and she's not about to come back. I know; we talked on the phone last night. She likes to call me when she's drunk. I'd leave now if it didn't mean having an uncomfortable conversation with my career counselor. She'll be proud I followed protocol and that I asked my dad about moving back in with him to focus on school full time. I may not be able to talk sense into Cassie, but I can become a paramedic as fast as possible, someone ready and capable if Cassie's heart stops or a jealous guy takes his fists to her or she loses another fingertip. Next time after they load her into the ambulance, I won't be standing on the sidewalk, watching it pull away. I'll be in there at her side—me, Mandy Ann Johnson—the one with the high voltage paddles, or at least the CPR.

IT'S HARD OUT HERE
FOR A PIMP

"SHE THREW A BEER at my head," my brother says. We're sitting on his balcony looking at other balconies, other people's underwear drying on clotheslines.

"That's a waste."

"Then she picked up the bottle of Jack and threatened to break her own face. Said she'd call the cops and tell them I did it." These are the women my brother attracts. The last one wore stripper heels to Christmas dinner.

I tell him he needs to document everything, note all the dates and times, and I take my cell from my purse and show him. "Hit the microphone button and talk. It's that easy." He pulls a beer from the cooler at his side and I keep on: leave her, change your locks, lay off the sauce.

"Yeah, totally," he says, "I'll totally think about it." Then he hawks a loogie over the railing. It's day one of my week back home.

At my mom's house *Dancing with the Stars* is on. I spill about Curtis during a commercial break and my mom shakes her head. "He dates just like someone with LD," which is short for learning disabilities.

"More like VD," I say, because what do learning disabilities have to do with it? In her bedroom there are three shelves of self-help books.

"You mean STDs."

"Actually, it's STIs now."

When Curtis had gonorrhea, he called it *the burn of love.* "I got the burn of love!" he said, poking me in the ribs. "But it's all good—just part of being a pimp." He was forty-years-old at the time.

"This one's meaner and smarter and he's in trouble," I say.

She says, "Let go and let God."

She says, "This too shall pass."

She says, "Can you turn up the TV?"

A few days later Curtis turns forty-three at a downtown bar. I show up and do my part; I mingle, I eat bean dip, I let his dentist hit on me and then pitch me Invisalign. There's a clinking of glasses and we listen as Curtis professes his love for the face-breaker, their fight already forgotten. They dance to a hair band ballad while the rest of us watch, and then they disappear into the bathroom.

"It's an '80s party," he says when I smear a spot of powder off his lip.

He dances over and gropes two women who are posing for a picture, his idea of photo-bombing, and that's when I can't take anymore. I walk with my jelly shoes and wave of bangs to a different bar, one I frequented in my twenties, so I can swallow a pitcher of margaritas in peace, smoke a half pack of cigarettes even though I no longer smoke. The bartender, a mom tattoo on his arm, tells me to name three things I'm thankful for. I say: bars that don't observe the smoking ordinance, Dolly Parton on the juke box, running into no one I know. He says, I got one too: someone like you I can talk to. And then he stands there with the hint of a smile.

In my hometown it finds me—in line at the coffee shop, picking up dry cleaning for my mom, getting an oil change. It starts, "Curtis was *so* wasted last night..." and anything comes next: slurred karaoke, nudity at the pool hall, one or more pissed off women, public breakdancing, shots of tequila, angry woman's boyfriend, threats, more threats, bloody lips, police, jail.

The day after his birthday the story came courtesy of Brandon

Schwartz, high school track athlete turned electrician. I ran into him buying shoes. It went: "Holy shit, after you left—ahaha—he moonwalked on the bar—a-haw-ha—then his hand was in her—hahaha—they shoved his head in the toilet."

I wasn't thinking anything when I curled my fingers into a fist and flung it at him. It came natural, like undressing for that bartender.

"Ahaha," I said and shook my hand.

Brandon said nothing, just looked at me hard like he wished I wasn't a woman.

At my mom's I put my hand on ice, my knuckles hot and stinging. "The sting of love," I tell my brother when my mom passes me the phone.

He says, "Now you the pimp, dog!"

"Right," I say. "I'm the pimp."

He brags on about his party but I don't hear it. I'm feeling a rawness in my throat, from the cigarettes maybe, feeling my throat constricting by the second until my breath stops entirely. And I sit there. And it's not that I can't relax, inhale again if I wanted to, it's that not breathing has its promise too, the burning in my lungs overtaking the pain in my hand.

"Sis," he says, "are you there?"

THE PULL

THAT TIME my dad took me camping by the Eel River at the Fortuna KOA. As we lay under the stars with the fire dying, he told me people eat spiders in their sleep—hundreds in a lifetime. They crawl toward the smell. "Don't be a mouth-breather," he said, and then he rolled over.

That time we flew to Tacoma to visit Grandma. I pressed my cheek to the window, prayed against the turbulence, its sticky grip. Stepping onto the tarmac after, the sky was darker, for the hive of planes above us, I thought, buzzing up there as we drove off, as we kicked a soccer ball in the park, as we waited for grandma's poodle to pee on weeds.

"Dad," I said unable to see through the clouds, "how much does a plane weigh?"

That time with my dad's girlfriend and her stack of black cotton candy hair. She set me on a barstool in front of the bathroom mirror and sprayed and bobby-pinned and teased a blond tornado from my head. "Why doesn't everyone wear her hair like this?" I asked. She said because that old lady died, the one whose hair was home to a black widow. They found the woman dead in her bed, found two tiny punctures on her scalp and an egg sack behind her ear.

That time my dad discovered my tampons under the bathroom sink. He put me in his truck and drove. Didn't say why or where we were going. When he spoke, out by the Brussels sprout fields, he said, "You need to understand: If you get pregnant, I'll kill whoever did it to you." He said, "For every life you add, I'll take one away. Keep things even." He turned the truck around and drove to Safeway, picked up some hamburger meat and ice cream.

That time in Big Sur with my boyfriend. Driving a thread of road that stitched the edge of a mountain. Him with that look, his hand dragging up my thigh. He didn't feel the pull of the ocean below, the slight drift of our car when I looked back. He didn't thrash in our tent each morning when the same dream spun its reel: the screeching of metal against the guardrail, our Datsun flipping over and cartwheeling down, the slap of the ocean and the slow sucking under, the both of us each millisecond wondering, Am I alive? Am I still alive?

CLIFFS

IN THE PARKING LOT on West Cliff Drive her dad sat on the
back bumper of their chartreuse station wagon and rubbed a puck of wax
in small, methodic circles across the surfboard on his lap. She finger-
crocheted in the back seat where he had tossed the wax's packaging. *Sex
Wax* is what it said. She wound her yellow yarn tight around her fingertip
and felt it go hot.

Before throwing his board into the water and plummeting in
himself, her dad stationed her on the bench on the cliff. She watched the
swells roll in, watched men like seals in their black suits straddling their
boards. A handful at a time, belly down on their wax, paddled to catch
what they hoped would spill into a ride. Her dad waved to her every so
often. It was better than leaving her home alone.

What she remembers now: that first day turning into many, turning into time served. The smell of sewage. Seal-men lobbing punches when they kerned too closely. The company of her mother's letters. The ball of wax she would mold into a perfect heart, then smash flat with the side of her fist.

VISITOR, TRANSISTOR

I'VE WORKED at the video store for three months, and I know all of
the customers already because everyone is a regular. If you aren't a regular,
you don't come here. You go to Blockbuster and rent Blu-rays or DVDs.
Only regulars still rent VHS.

Movie posters wallpaper the windows, so it could be January
outside or June, but I wouldn't know. Birds chirping, an old lady slipping
on ice, a spider rappelling from the awning, I wouldn't know.

My boss has all these rules, like no cell phones or anything
resembling a computer. I write your number on my hand before work,
because when I get sick of watching *Lethal Weapon* or *Men in Black*, I call
you from the phone on the wall. It's one reason I know how a leashed dog
feels.

When non-regulars wander in, I count the beats until they stop smiling. They push backward out the door, eyes averted, sayonara, poof! From then on, we are a vacant lot. We are a field of brown weeds.

Today I call you and say how working alone is a drag. Your voice crackles and pops, and from the phone, a white noise rushing.

"Hello," I say. "Can you hear me? Are you there?"

"Right here," says a man at the counter, a man I've never seen before. He's standing right there and looking right at me.

I hang up the phone and his eyes follow. I cross to the register and they track me still. I'm asking, "Can I help you? Are you lost?"

At first he is a mannequin, his trench coat, his fedora, his eyes clacking from left to right, but then he walks around the counter and leans me up against the wall.

"I'm going to take my time," he says.

I say, "It's been slow all day."

I should probably be offended, because let's face it, he's older and at least twenty pounds overweight. But you're gone from the phone, and his breath on my neck is a jungle. I smell large felines and photosynthesis and feel the tickle of a millipede. A siren sounds from somewhere outside. Or maybe from the movie playing. Either way, I prepare my mouth. I tell him, "Please, please, please, turn it up."

THE TRUE LOVE OF
MAGNUM P.I.

MY MOM THINKS Magnum P.I. is a babe. She likes his dimples
and mustache, and the red Ferrari doesn't hurt either. Not that a car is a
body part, but it helps, like the jeans my mom says slim her hips. I look at
him and see a bunch of hair bushes: two above his eyes, one under his
nose, a thicket on his head and chest. I watch the show because my mom
makes popcorn and we drink Coke and burp.

After a few weeks I realize Magnum looks like my dad, except my
dad is balding and stockier, and he shakes when he lifts anything heavy.
My dad is private too, though not very investigative. He says there's a
reason I flunked Home Economics: *Attention.* And why I dance to the *Best
of Blondie* with the curtains open: *Attention.* But he doesn't ask; he doesn't
get to the bottom of it. There are no dimples when he says it because he's

not smiling. Back at my mom's I mention the resemblance, but of course she disagrees one hundred percent. When it comes to my dad, she always exaggerates her percents.

We keep watching and I start to see a wisdom in the show, especially when Magnum discovers his Vietnamese wife is alive after years of believing her dead. He tries to save her from her current lover who is evil and also Asian, but she disappears in the end, before Magnum can drink Mai Tais with her or fight with her or know what her hips look like out of her jeans. It is true love always.

After that episode I begin experimenting with tragedy, mostly on the weekends at my dad's house. I hang around the 7-Eleven long enough for him to think I have been abducted. *I* would have thought I had been abducted. I dabble in bulimia and then in bullying, but neither feel very good; I don't stick with them for long. I sneak liquor from his liquor cabinet but must be good at pouring only a sip from each bottle because I don't get a talking to.

It is not until I puke the liquor cabinet mix onto his living room carpet that he approaches me with any sense of urgency. He grabs me by the shoulders and rushes me to the deck where I continue all over the bougainvillea. Later I remember how he rested his hand on my back as I sweated and heaved. It wasn't true love always, his hand hadn't stayed for long, but I remember it felt warm and strong. I remember I felt steady.

I'm watching even closer now, taking notes, planning bigger. Alcohol is kids stuff, really. I'm thinking shark attack or helicopter crash.

I'm thinking high-speed car chase. I'm thinking this house I am sitting in, burning.

DAVID HASSELHOFF IS
FROM BALTIMORE

YOU ARRIVE FINALLY on the California coast, and even though this is northern California, you're expecting tan, leggy blondes and barrel-chested surfers. You're expecting red swimsuits and lifeguard stations and blinding white sand. You've brought your own red swimsuit and you're expecting California to deliver.

Here's what you get instead: jagged cliffs covered in seagull shit. You get wet wind. You get big-armed bearded men who ride Harley's, and tie-dyed, wrinkled women who smell like lavender. You get a runny nose and damp feet and an icy ocean that couldn't care less about red swimsuits. It says fuck you red swimsuit, I am busy tearing at land. I will tear until I reach the Atlantic.

This is the news after 1,062 quiet miles—after one divorce, two yard sales, four months of double shifts, and a spate of Coors Light hangovers. With no idea how many hours' drive it is to palm trees, you stop at the roadhouse and get a room upstairs, #7, with a lighthouse quilt. You get shared bathrooms at the end of the hall with a basket of toiletries from previous guests. This is better than standing in a Wal-Mart in Montana choosing a brand of hairspray. Which is least likely to catch fire? You are happy not to have to decide. You are happy for leftover Aqua-net.

As a girl you stood in that Wal-Mart in Montana pulling at your mother's skirt. You watched as she set a box of Life back on the shelf, shut her eyes and breathed out, "California." You let go and tried to catch the word in your hands, tried to hold it between you like it was something you could share.

Downstairs at the bar you find a book of matches with "Mike" and a phone number penciled inside the flap. You head outside and use one of the matches to light a cigarette, a Virginia Slim, which you feel you deserve for having come a long way. You dial Mike and when he answers you say, "Convertibles."

He says, "Hello? Who's this?"

You say, "I see cars but no convertibles. I see a chapel and a feed store and a community center and three teenagers walking to the cliffs, and not a one of them is rollerblading."

He says, "You're still at the bar. Stay there, I'm coming."

He arrives and he is handsome. Blue eyes, black hair. He is a big-armed, bearded man, and he is looking for someone else. You show him the matches and ask if you'll do.

"Let's walk," he says, and the two of you head out through a field to the edge of the ocean. You tell him you are not trying to find your mother, and he shrugs like it's not for him to say. He says, ""What I know is this: the bartender, from Nebraska, will let you smoke inside during the Tuesday night pool tournaments. The cook, from Kentucky, will make grits on cold days even though they're not on the menu. The taxi driver, from South Dakota, drives drunk after 7:00 pm. And I," he says, "don't know dick about surfboards, but I can mix you a margarita. I can shine your shoulders with oil."

"Nebraska?" you say. "Kentucky? South Dakota?" You say, "I'm trying to find California."

He scratches his beard. "Which is what?" he says. "Hollywood? David Hasselhoff? How about you ask him where he's from."

The non-rollerblading teenagers begin setting off fireworks, and you try to remember if today is a holiday. Mike's face turns orange, purple, white as he watches. You tell yourself you'll kiss him when the number of explosions reaches 101, the highway you're to take south in the morning. You're counting *84, 85, 86,* and you're smoking faster and laughing harder and he's daring you to strip down and wade in.

"Go all the way," you say, and you unbutton and unzip, push down and pull off.

Mike whistles as you tramp over sand that might as well be snow, your body illuminating under the bursts. You push into that angry ocean, the cold whipping your thighs, cementing your lungs, your mouth sucking the night for air. An oncoming wave readies to bury your head, and your arms butterfly forward, your feet kick free of land.

ACKNOWLEDGMENTS

Thank you to the editors who previously published the following stories: "She Could Maybe Lift a Car" Monkeybicycle, "The Rumor Was" Hobart, "Because I Wanted to Write You a Pop Song" Wigleaf, "Ferris Wheel" Word Riot, "Crash" Atticus Review, "Four Hands" [PANK], "Betty" The Los Angeles Review, "Thirty-Four" Revolver, "Don Johnson Is Not Your Man" Wigleaf, "Werewolves" Spork, "Usually on Sunday" Necessary Fiction, "Bonus Round" No Tokens, "Wine Country" Wigleaf (as a postcard), "Lesbionic" The Stockholm Review of Literature, "It's Hard Out Here for a Pimp" Whiskeypaper, "The Pull" Split Lip Magazine, "Visitor, Transistor" Paper Darts, "The True Love of Magnum P.I." Sundog Lit, "David Hasselhoff Is from Baltimore" Smokelong Quarterly

Shiny Gold Stars of Thanks to: Amanda Miska (ace editor and hustler), Shirin Bridges, Amanda Ault, Erin Brookey Roeder, Tex Clark, Jennifer Akiyama, Michael David Lukas, Jen Licon-Conner, David Vernor, Janet Fogel, Kim Miskowicz, Vince Gotera, Georgia Bellas, Lindsay Hunter, my Santa Rosa salon (Leilani, Dani, Jessica, Rachel & Dave), Guy's Group (especially Tricia, Carol, Jim, & Wray), the Elizabeth George Foundation, the Corkscrew Wine Bar, and the faculty and students at the Northwest Institute of Literary Arts.

All the Stars in the Sky to: Ken Prosser, Jake Prosser, and Brian Vernor, for their unwavering love and support.

Cover art by Kim Miskowicz, a visual artist based in Oakland, California. Her work is based on the response to material and data overload creating breaks in continuous thoughts, similar to a building that obstructs a view of a simple horizon. See more of her work at: **kimmiskowicz.com**.

ABOUT THE AUTHOR

Kara Vernor's fiction has appeared in *Gigantic Sequins, PANK, No Tokens, The Los Angeles Review*, and elsewhere. She has been a Best Small Fictions finalist, a Pushcart Prize nominee, and a Mendocino Coast Writers' Conference Estelle Frank Fellow. She is currently an Elizabeth George Foundation scholar at the Northwest Institute of Literary Arts, and she cohosts *Get Lit*, a quarterly reading series in San Francisco's North Bay.

NOW AVAILABLE FROM

Split Lip Press

I Am the Oil of the Engine of the World
by Jared Yates Sexton

forget me / hit me / let me drink great quantities of clear, evil liquor
by Katie Schmid

The State Springfield Is In
by Tom C. Hunley

For more info about the press and our titles, please visit:

WEBSITE: www.splitlippress.com
FACEBOOK: facebook.com/splitlippress
TWITTER: @splitlippress

AND DISCOVER MORE IN

Find great literature, music, fine art and film by visiting:

WEBSITE: www.splitlipmagazine.com
FACEBOOK: facebook.com/splitlipmagazine
TWITTER: @splitlippress

CPSIA information can be obtained
at www.ICGtesting.com
Printed in the USA
LVOW12s0527110418

573050LV00002BA/315/P